After the Rapture

Nancy Stohlman

Mason Jar Press | *Baltimore, MD*

Cover design and layout by Ian Anderson.

This book is set in FF Meta Serif.

Publishded by
Mason Jar Press
Baltimore, MD

Printed by Spencer Printing in Honesdale, PA.

Learn more about Mason Jar Press at masonjarpress.com.

for Nick

After the Rapture

Part One

Before the Rapture, a bad thing happened, and the people were horrified, and they cried, and they played the details over and over like a particularly painful heartbreak. And someone decided that a memorial should be built, and everyone should wear red, and once a year everyone wore red and remembered the bad thing and it seemed right.

The next time a bad thing happened, people decided it was only fitting to designate another color—white this time—and people wore white, and some people wore red and white together to show how the two bad things were connected and that also seemed right.

But the bad things kept happening. Soon the primary colors were gone—then the secondary colors. The newest tragedies were forced to come up with creative coloring like teal or lavender and soon it expanded beyond colors—people in mourning for a specific tragedy could either wear the color or buy a bracelet made of that color and some people had 10–15 bracelets going up their arm until it was pointed out that the bracelets weren't produced in an environmentally friendly manner and then people got rid of all the bracelets and tried to go back to the colors, but even the colors didn't work now, because every color was affiliated with a tragedy, and if you were wearing, say, lime-green pants, but you didn't know which bad thing was being mourned in lime green, then you might be called a poser and accused of trivializing other people's suffering.

And still the bad things increased until there were several bad things every week, and new symbols had to be devised to express your horror: praying hands and beating hearts and hugging arms you could send electronically or turn into magnetic bumper stickers for cars or bicycles and you could also swap your electronic picture frame to one specially made to announce your devastation at the new bad thing, but sometimes another bad thing would happen on that very same day and you would not know if you should keep the original picture frame to mourn the first bad thing or if you should update to mourn the most recent bad thing, and those who updated would be called insensitive by the ones who had not yet finished mourning the first bad thing.

It got to the point where the bad things had to compete with the other bad things, and a thing that would have been pretty bad back in the days of the primary colors was now almost ignored. And people abandoned the picture frames but they didn't know which symbols to use, now, which led them to create new symbols like baking cakes in the shapes of tragedies that needed to be mourned, and sometimes they traveled to the locations of the bad things just to feel the awfulness more acutely and they became jumpy like children in volatile households who are trying to read the signs and see the next bad thing approaching and so sometimes they would see regular things as bad things and jump at the sight of prayer hands or beating hearts or hugging arms until they became numb and the bad things kept happening but they were out of colors, and out of ideas, and so, eventually, they did nothing.

* * * * *

I went into Walmart for a bag of ice, something I never do because I don't like Walmart, and I don't like ice, and the ice was of course located next to the wall of Missing Persons and there I was: missing. My picture, the one I got for my passport last year, was hanging next to an artist's rendition of what I would look like now, one year later, which was basically the same but with longer bangs, which was exactly what I did look like. I stood there confused, reading my height and weight. It said I was last seen in Walmart one year ago, probably when I also needed ice.

There was a number for information, so I called. A woman answered. Missing Persons Hotline, she said.

I want to report a sighting of a missing person, I said.

Where?

Here, at Walmart. It's me. I mean, the missing person is me. I'm not missing, I'm right here. I'm not sure what's going on.

She sounded unconcerned. Well, it definitely says you're missing. For nearly 11 months. Where have you been?

I haven't been anywhere, I said.

What have you been doing?

I've been, you know, just doing regular stuff. Who reported me as missing?

All information from sources is kept anonymous, she said. You must understand why. People might be afraid to come forward if they had to give their names.

Well can you report me as not missing now?

Sure. We'll need you to come down to the police station for fingerprint matching first, though.

I showed up at the station and they sent me to the Missing Persons wing. I sat in the lobby and it seemed everyone was staring, looking at my picture on the wall and then back at me. One woman finally approached the receptionist and said in a half-whisper—I want to report a missing person sighting.

I can hear you, I said. I'm not even missing. There's been a mistake.

They took my fingerprints, confirmed my identity, and then thanked me for coming forward. It's because of citizens like you that we're able to recover people who might stay missing, she said, handing me a wet wipe for my inky fingers.

I went back to Walmart a week later to see if they had removed my poster but it had only been updated: Last seen in Walmart. Please call with any information.

* * * * *

According to prophecy, the Rapture would begin when the faithful were lifted into the air—two friends walking side by side and then *poof!* one disappears. But it didn't happen that way at all.

Instead, after it was discovered that a man had successfully lived in a Paris airport for more than 20 years, the people started buying airline tickets with no intention of ever arriving at a destination. After so many years exposed, of having one's life documented, one's daily moods broadcast, one's most tragic moments shared and reshared, the people craved anonymity. The duty-free areas were technically nowhere, a no-man's land between countries, and the Asian airports with their rental sleeping pods were particularly attractive. Soon there were coin showers, food court punch cards, and chapels that changed denominations every hour. In an airport no one gave a shit who you were, where you were going, or whether your life was working out according to plans. In the sweet blur of movement, the people were finally able to disappear.

* * * * *

Before the Rapture, all the romaine lettuce was quietly removed from grocery store shelves as if it had never been there. Thankfully there were other varieties of lettuce like green leaf and butter lettuce, but it was alarming to see those big empty spaces in the produce aisles like a mouth full of missing teeth.

Then the ground beef, and that hit a little harder. Then the chicken cholera, as it came to be called, which affected both chickens and eggs and surprised no one. Then porcine herpes, which was called the "most serious infraction against humankind yet."

At this point vegans were feeling pretty smug, even without the lettuce, until locusts attacked the wheat and soy and corn crops, leaving them withered in the fields.

People continued to cautiously buy from the pre-packaged aisle until a report confirmed what we'd all suspected for years—the hormones in plastic were changing the gene structures of children and teens, and women were now hitting menopause at age 20, and men were growing breasts and bleeding from their asses. So all that had to go.

Then there was arsenic in the rice. Then toxic cinnamon. Then Coca-Cola dumped half a million gallons of soda into the landfills as if disposing of evidence.

And then, as quietly as it began, everything was returned to the grocery store shelves as if there had never been any lapse. As if we'd been dreaming the other. Now the strawberries were as big as lemons, the steaks were perfectly marbled, the roasted turkeys were glazed like the lips of a porn star, and the whipped cream dollops were flawless angels landing on a pillow of key lime.

It was only later we wondered how we could have been so stupid. Lab rats will consume enough poison to kill themselves if it's fed to them slowly and has a pleasant taste; a frog will allow itself to be boiled alive if it's done in incrementally slow amounts, so in the end we did it to ourselves.

* * * * *

Rapture Quiz: Which World Dictator Are You Related To?

Is it Mussolini? Fidel Castro? Idi Amin? Saddam Hussein? Mao Zedong? Which cold-blooded dictator are YOU related to? Take this short quiz! Mail a DNA sample plus $25 to this address in Utah and find out!

They're always trying to get us to send DNA samples. I have friends who won't play these games—my friends who won't play these games all have vast conspiracies around what they're really doing with all that DNA in Utah. They're tracking us all the time anyway, my friend who lives inside a school bus says. I don't even have a King Soopers card. I don't want them to have my DNA and I definitely don't want them to know what I buy at the grocery store.

I don't usually fall for these but the Which World Dictator Are You Related To? quiz was just too tempting, so I spat in the little tube and drove around until I found one of those big old-fashioned mailboxes and dropped the box in the navy-blue void.

Four to six weeks later, I get a knock on the door. We're here to deliver your quiz results and your clone, the FedEx guy says. Just sign here.

I didn't order a clone.

You signed the Terms and Conditions, he says.

But everyone signs those.

Stating you will be responsible for the maintenance of any clones created from the DNA process.

He leads the clone to the door. She's naked and smells funny.

Don't I even get to find out which world dictator I'm related to?

Of course. Your results were: Franco! he says, holding up a sheet with a picture of Franco and some biographical information.

I wasn't expecting Franco. I was thinking Pinochet or maybe even Stalin.

Everyone wants Stalin, but that's not mathematically possible, my clone answers, handing me my results.

* * * * *

Before the Rapture, the jellyfish began multiplying until there were tens of thousands of jellyfish per square mile and the seas became slippery with their weird bodies.

Then Lake Michigan turned red, which people thought was probably due to pollution or maybe too many birth control pills dumped down the toilet, but then the jellyfish started appearing in the lake, too, which made no sense because it was a freshwater lake, but there they were, thousands of jellyfish undulating like plastic bags under the water.

Then came the frogs, hopping down Michigan Avenue, and people were screaming and running, and squashed frog carcasses smeared the streets, and buses tried to swerve, and all the people carrying concealed weapons (which turned out to be a lot of people!) became like movie star vigilantes but they weren't such good shots so frog bodies were splattering everywhere and a bunch of regular people got shot, too.

Then came the thunderstorms of fire and hail, which caused the lake to boil and rise up and stain the shoreline red. People slipped on jellyfish like banana peels, then became feverish and contracted painful boils that burst into an oozing, communicable gel. Doctors were forced to use the rest of their snakebite antidote, which was unfortunate because there were also snakes in all the toilets, coiled up and hissing.

This went on for seven days and seven nights, and then on the eighth day the lake went back to normal and the skies cleared and all the frogs and snakes and boils disappeared, leaving only discarded jellyfish on the shore as a reminder. And a warning.

* * * * *

My invitation came in the mail: You're invited to our Fall Orgy! Please bring a dish to share!

The orgies started last month. Someone had decided we weren't getting any younger and we'd better see each other naked before it was too late. The first orgy was super awkward, and I ended up getting Jell-O stuck in my hair and down the back of my favorite coat.

I arrive at this week's orgy with my Tupperware and the intention of just saying hi and leaving. My friend opens the door dressed as Hugh Heffner. You're here, he says. He touches my elbow and holds it there a beat too long. I'm so glad you could make it.

There are drinks in the kitchen and snacks in the living room. The fall theme is reinforced in every room with plastic gourds and an actual pile of leaves.

I can't stay, I say to our hostess.

Just a little bit, she says, refilling my daiquiri.

Eventually the host calls us all into the living room and hands out bathrobes. So everyone take a break, because we have a special guest here today who wants to invite us all to his condo in...the Bahamas!

No, *your* condo in the Bahamas!

We clap awkwardly as a guy wearing glasses and a sweater vest comes to the front of the living room and begins to tell us about time share opportunities in the Bahamas, complete with a PowerPoint presentation showing different floor plans and cost brackets. When he's finished he calls my friend back up:

We love our time share, my friend says. It's one of the best purchases we've ever made.

Did you hear that folks? One of the best purchases he has *ever* made. You can sit down now, Time Share Guy says, pushing my friend back toward his chair. Because I'd like to give each of you an opportunity to discuss your own personal condo needs with one of our happiness specialists.

They divide us into groups and lead us off to different parts of the house. My group ends up in the back bedroom, where several salespeople block the door. I know what you're thinking, Time Share Guy says—you just want to sit through the spiel, get some free stuff, and then get back to your orgy. But our company doesn't work that way. Before anyone leaves this room, someone will be purchasing a time share condo.

The door is blocked by two more bouncers. There's a pile of purses and wallets in the middle of the room. How about the first person who signs up for a time share gets to go home? And for the rest of you, I have several PowerPoint presentations as well as a TED Talk we can watch. He lifts a faux leather purse from the pile by its strap like a dead rat. We have a winner, he announces. Whose purse is this?

No one answers.

He opens it up and goes for the wallet. Jackie? Who's Jackie? No one says anything. Well, I guess we could just take all these credit cards and create a new identity.

No, no, it's mine, Jackie says, coming forward with her head hung.

Jackie, you're about to be the proud owner of a time share condo. Let's give her a round of applause, everyone.

One by one we're all called forward and one by one we sign a 20-year contract for a time share condo. As we're leaving, our host and hostess stand at the door handing us little parting gifts in paper bags tied with ribbons. *I'm sorry,* he mouths.

* * * * *

When St. Joe, Missouri was announced as the Best Place Ever to watch the Rapture, the people felt chosen. Not since Lady Gaga had come to Kansas City had they felt so special.

No one was exactly sure what would happen. Some thought it would be a fiery ball dropping from the sky, or ash blocking out the sun until they all choked, or floods, earthquakes, hurricanes or volcanic eruptions. As the day of final judgement drew closer, Motel 6 jacked up its prices to $800 a night, the porn shop repaved the parking lot, and gun shops ran out of both guns and ammo. Red Lobster, the nicest restaurant in town, put all-you-can-eat Rapture Scallops on the menu. Dunkin Donuts, overwhelmed by it all, just said fuck it and shut down.

Half a million people descended upon St. Joe. They came with Rapture glasses, Rapture t-shirts (*Prepare for the Rapture with Pepsi!*) and Rapture key chains, booking out the KOA and every hotel room in town. When all the grass was claimed, the people started pitching tents right on the concrete. Dan Rather showed up in an RV. Matthew McConaughey and Gwyneth Paltrow were spotted on a rooftop eating hot dogs and raving about untouched Americana.

The day of the Rapture, everyone was ready. Some had UV glasses, some had hazmat suits, some were naked and meditating, some boarded up their windows and the tornado sirens sounded for good measure and everyone waited outside, watching the sky. Crowding the streets and waving fireball pompoms and trying to shove Rapture pancakes in their mouths.

As the Rapture was about to begin the sky filled with thick black clouds. It will blow over, they assured each other, unconvinced.

Then a rumor swept through the town that Beatrice, just one hour north, was a much better place to see the Rapture. People dropped their pancakes mid-bite, fled to their cars and flooded the highways, which became gridlocked almost instantly for 40 miles in either direction, leaving St. Joe like an exhausted whore.

Some that remained put on their UV glasses anyway, just in case, and they were lucky because hundreds of people went blind without seeing a thing.

* * * * *

I'm driving. At first the other car is just a blur of silver, nothing I pay attention to. There's a lush grassy median separating the north and south highways and two gray headlights like dull eyes coming diagonally across the green. Something's wrong. The realization hits first and then the quickening. And then the knowing. Followed by the impact.

* * * * *

I awake to swirling dust and strange floating silence. Faces look
through the remains of windows spidered but held in place—We
saw everything, the faces are saying, and now I hear the first
muffled ambulance sirens in the far distance. Did the airbag go
off? someone asks and there's a blood-speckled airbag deflated
across my chest. Can you move? I can feel both my legs up to
the waist and I seem to have my teeth, and the sirens are loud
now, and a lady pushes a stack of business cards through the
broken glass—We're all witnesses!—and now the windows crowd
with the faces of men in uniforms: What's your name? Where do
you live? Can you tell me what happened? She's coherent! they
say, just hold on we're going to get you out of there—and now
they're ripping off what's left of the hood of my car with a giant
tool and I'm being covered with a sheet—Hang on! they say over
the sound of glass shattering, pieces landing on top of me, then
the sounds of metal twisting and squeaking as they try to pry
the door off—One, two three, again!—they're rocking the car in
unison with their weight and then the door releases and I fall
back into their arms and I'm lifted into the light.

* * * * *

The scissors slide easily through the thick denim of my favorite blue jeans, from ankle to waist, ankle to waist, as one leg then the other falls away. He slices up the middle of my cotton shirt like tissue paper, unwrapping me, my pink Victoria's Secret bra snipped and spilling to the ground.

Are you having trouble breathing? he asks with kind brown eyes.

A little, on one side, I whisper.

We'll be there soon, he says, gently placing the oxygen mask as the ambulance sirens rattle the warm evening air.

* * * * *

The doctor is addressing the tour group: The lung is collapsing, see. We're going to put a small incision here and get the chest tube in.

You're going to feel some pressure, he whispers.

And then I'm crucified.

Hear that hiss. That's the trapped air in the lung releasing, he says to cheers and applause as a flock of birds exits my chest cavity, circles the room in formation, and flies out the window.

* * * * *

When I wake from surgery, groggy, head rolling, I have a Barbie arm. It has a round plastic shoulder in a smooth socket and a bright shiny plastic finish. The arm is bent at a 45-degree angle and comes with a hole to hold a microphone or a cooking spoon or a wine glass.

I thought you were putting pins in my elbow, I say to the doctor when he comes to check on me.

We were, but your insurance only pays for 22 minutes of surgery and pins take about 38, so when we realized we weren't going to make it we switched to Plan B, he says. These are actually better in many ways, since you wouldn't get full range of motion anyway. He thumps my plastic, shiny bicep. Durable as hell. Patients end up loving them.

My Barbie arm lies there at a funny angle. All the fingers are fused together and the tips of the nails are painted.

I stay there for a week but the doctor doesn't visit again and won't return my phone calls so I finally follow him to his car one evening. This isn't working, I say, my arm sticking out like a polio-stricken child. I need my old arm back.

Your old arm was already recycled, he says. They come on Tuesdays so if you would have told me sooner I could have salvaged it. Perhaps if you met the right partner it would make you feel better?

I'm already married.

Well that won't last long, he says. Especially if that's your pleasure hand, if you know what I mean. He pops a lollipop in his mouth. I'm sure you do, he adds. I'm sure you are very entertaining.

* * * * *

Things that happened during the Rapture: A group of people decided to stare right at it without looking away until their retinas burned out and a white milky film covered their eyes and they became like strange blind sages and soothsayers, wandering around making predictions about things they couldn't have possibly known were going to happen and yet, remarkably, did.

* * * * *

Rapture Hotline: Where are you calling from?

Cody, Wyoming. I'm pretty sure me and my friend just saw Mary in the Slurpee machine.

What is your location?

The 7-Eleven by the Walmart on the way out of town.

And what exactly happened?

Well, my friend was getting cherry and I was getting lemon-lime and then he was like what the hell is that? And this lady was floating above the Slurpee machine.

Describe the lady.

You know, it was Mary. Like God's Mary. She was white, with blue robes. She was wearing glasses, which was weird, but other than that it looked like Mary.

Did she say anything?

No, but she was definitely more over the cherry side so I switched flavors. We both felt really happy there, just watching her.

And then what happened?

She disappeared but then on the ground right at our feet we found $80 in 20s, all folded up.

We'll send someone right away. Thanks for the tip!

* * * * *

I'm not sure why I need a vaginal exam, I say at my follow-up appointment.

It's just easier this way, he says. And I'll give you an IUD while I'm here. They have these new Swedish ones that last an extra three years. Are you a risk-taking sort of girl?

Listen, I just want my arm back, I say.

I told you I don't have it. But I can give you a plastic anything, he adds. Even a plastic...you know.

* * * * *

After the Rapture, the people began a strange pilgrimage. They traveled from the broken cities, through streets littered with expired business cards, past billboards that had long ago stopped promising anything.

They walked over the Rocky Mountains and across the desert toward Salt Lake City, Utah and the Very First Kentucky Fried Chicken, the one started by the actual Colonel Sanders when "fried" was still part of the name. It seemed pointless to care about things like cholesterol now; those who had been vegetarians and those who didn't eat fried foods journeyed side by side.

The route to the Very First Kentucky Fried Chicken was marked by cairns and totems. People interviewed along the way said they felt a certain calm on the months-long journey, that it was good to be away from the normal pressures of daily life and just be one with the scorching 100-degree temps of the high Utah desert, where understandably a certain number of pilgrims would not make it and their bodies would be left as they fell, adorned by the pilgrims to follow like roadside altars.

For those who arrived, a large yet modest daily buffet awaited so pilgrims would not be forced to choose between original and extra crispy chicken, and there was both brown and white gravy and some even claimed to find a real lump in the mashed potatoes. And the fountain drinks ran freely and people shared their sporks under the grinning life-sized Colonel Sanders, decorated with beads and sunglasses and candles and smudge sticks and good luck fortunes left in thanks for a safe journey.

And then the people, desperate to avoid what came next, took their chicken bones and kept walking. They walked west for many days toward the setting sun until they reached the edge. But no matter how many bones they threw, they couldn't fill the great, yawning silence that followed them back to the remains of their ruined lives.

* * * * *

After the Rapture, I decide to buy a tiny house. The Realtor meets me in the driveway.

That's not a tiny house, I say. That's a Barbie house.

You say Barbie house, I say tiny house, the Realtor says. Wait until you see the inside.

He opens the flimsy door. The walls are made of pink vinyl with drawings of bookshelves and framed family photos and a two-dimensional crayon television. That's for easy collapsing, he says. The whole house can fold up into this suitcase—he holds up a pink suitcase—which most people find extremely convenient.

The fridge door can open, he adds, opening and closing the door several times. And your oven comes with a roast chicken already cooked.

It looks delicious, I lie.

Yes, it does. The house comes with wine glasses but no actual wine, of course.

Of course.

In the bedroom is a walk-in closet with tiny hangers and a vinyl bed that folds down from the wall. A cat sits unmoving on the bed.

I'm allergic to cats, I say.

Oh, you won't be allergic to this one, he says.

As we stand there, one of the vinyl walls starts to buckle and he pushes it back into place.

The best part about this house are the amenities, he says, taking me outside to the carport and a pink Cadillac. The car comes with the house.

Wow, that is a perk, I say.

Yes it is. You may be asked to sell some Mary Kay skin care products, but I think you'll find the moisturizer is great. Hold on, he says, checking his phone. I need to take this.

While he steps to the corner where the two vinyl walls meet, I look in the closet. A candy-striper outfit, a pink tennis outfit. A pink ball gown. Pink leather boots.

Good news, he says, I've been authorized to throw in the Barbie ice cream maker—it makes real ice cream and other frozen treats.

Hmmm.

And the Barbie helicopter and landing pad.

Well I have to be honest—it wasn't quite what I had in mind, I say. I was thinking of a tiny house made of wood or something. You know, like they have on TV.

Oh, you won't see a house like this on TV, he agrees. And actually, you won't find another house like this in the entire state—most of them have been recalled.

Okay, let me think about it.

Don't take too long, he says. A deal like this won't last forever.

* * * * *

After the Rapture, the people voted to drain Loch Ness—the infamous lake in the Scottish Highlands that may or may not have contained a monster—and find out the goddamn truth once and for all.

The draining began on a Saturday. The water was channeled through makeshift valves and diverted north for 16 miles, all the way to the sea along carefully built irrigation ditches. By Saturday night the people were getting impatient; the lake emptied so slowly, like a clogged bathtub. Little by little, as the water table gradually lowered, travelers in the know began to arrive from all over Scotland, then the greater UK, then Europe to wait on the lakeshore edges, excited by every rock suddenly exposed. But the rocks always proved to be just rocks, and somehow the people already knew what was coming. They continued anyway. Soon people came from every part of the world, a steady influx to witness this slow draining of imagination, the small water of faith shrinking day after day until it became impossible to deny that the bottom of Loch Ness was covered with rocks and shells and abandoned furniture and clumps of waterlogged trash, and the people knew it was too late to put all the water back and pretend they hadn't seen the bottom, because even if the water returned, the monster would not.

* * * * *

I met Ken on the internet. Now he's sitting awkwardly in a Chipotle chair, waiting for me with toothy grin and unblinking eyes. We sort of shake hands.

I like your arm, he says as I sit down.

Thanks, I like your...skin. They give you a tan?

Yeah, it's called Summertime Ken, he says. I have a safari hat and sunglasses in the car.

He has a taco bowl in front of him but isn't eating. I'm not actually hungry, he says. You want to take a ride in my new Jungle Safari Jeep? He hasn't blinked or stopped smiling.

We take off and Ken's painted-on hair doesn't blow. There's a painted-on dog in the back seat. I just call him Buddy, Ken shouts as we drive. He keeps me less lonely.

Are we going to your house? I ask.

Funny you should mention that, he shouts over the wind. Maybe you haven't noticed there is no Ken Dream House. I've been eating condiments and living in a tent on the edge of town.

You're homeless?

No, I have a tent and Buddy here keeps me company at night.

But Buddy is a drawing.

Wow, he says, they gave you a helicopter pad. They didn't even give me the same color leg when mine was ripped out of the socket last year.

Listen Ken, I didn't ask for it to be this way.

Yeah, well, you do things your way and I'll do them mine, okay?

Ken is still smiling but silent.

* * * * *

After the Rapture, all the people were waking up, but I'm not sure what that meant, and I'm not even sure *they* knew what it meant, and I never trusted anyone who claimed to have woken up. My friend claimed to have woken up a few months ago but she still seems like a bitch to me. And even at Starbucks they would stare and if you weren't awake they wouldn't draw a heart in the latte foam.

I started to see someone about it privately because I was getting worried I should have woken up by now—if my neighbor, who loves NASCAR, was now awake as he had claimed when we were both at the mailbox on Thursday—Hey, guess what, I woke up! he said—then surely I should be awake.

But then a new movement started to discredit those who were awake, claiming there was no science behind it, after all, and "awake" was subjective, and by the way *what's wrong with sleep?* And pretty soon everyone claimed that lucid dreaming was more evolved, and people started sleeping 18 hours a day and taking classes where they would try to meet each other inside of dreams, and a new café called Asleep opened next to the Awake cafe and they served chamomile and valerian drinks and everything was cushioned and comfy and if you fell asleep anywhere, in class, on the train, people would assume you were on some sort of spiritual path.

And of course I talked to my guy again, because I didn't know if I should be awake or asleep now, and he said to become asleep while waking was the true goal.

Pretty soon a rock shattered the front glass of Asleep café and everyone assumed it was the awake folks, and some people thought it was a provocateur, an asleep person who wanted to frame the awakes and turn public opinion against them. Splinter groups further divided—those who claimed to be both asleep and awake as well as radical groups that never slept or never woke. And people had no idea who was awake and who was asleep and so they were afraid to interact at all.

What was left of the government called a state of emergency. Pretty soon all the awake people decided they should leave. So they all got on boats and trains and buses and left. And the asleep people felt sad they had no one to fight with and some of them wondered if maybe the awakes had been right all along and they tried it and woke up. While the people on the boats and trains, free from the pressure of always having to be awake, finally fell asleep.

Part Two

Sometimes I wake in the middle of the night and think my old arm is still there. Shhh, Ken says, pushing his plastic torso against my back. It's okay.

But it's not okay. It's definitely not okay.

So I file a Missing Property Report anyway, even if it's pointless, and they say they'll put out an alert but not to get my hopes up because yes, a certain number of body parts are recovered each year, but a certain number of them are never recovered either, and as soon as anything crosses the border it's especially hard to keep track of it.

I also post a Craigslist ad in the lost and found section and I receive many pictures of other body parts but not my arm.

I also make a large poster: *Reward: No Questions Asked.*

You better not put that, Ken says while I glue sparkles. And you better not put your home address—they might come for the other arm.

I return to Walmart and tape it on the wall of Missing Persons next to my original missing poster, which now has an addition:

Distinguishing Marks: Barbie arm.

In marker, someone has added a moustache and devil horns.

* * * * *

Day at the Beach Barbie!

Barbie and Ken get away from the hustle and bustle in this Day at the Beach Barbie brand fantasy play set! Your child can pack the Barbie Dream Car with picnic basket, umbrella and beach chairs! Barbie accessories include a fashionable French bathing suit, wide-brimmed sunhat (no sun damage here!), sunglasses and beach bag! Comes with palm trees and a Mexican hammock! [*Made in China*] Your child will love soaking up rays with Day at the Beach Barbie, who comes with a UV light that gives Barbie a real tan! [*UV tan lines are temporary and will fade after 30 mins. Warning: do not let children lay under UV light.*]

Oh look—here comes Lifeguard Ken! Is that a shark fin? Everyone out of the water! Let Ken rescue Barbie from the riptides and the undertow! This and more can happen as Ken performs CPR on Barbie and saves the day! [*Ken and friends sold separately.*]

* * * * *

Barbie Through the Years

1959:   *Barbie premieres at New York Toy Fair*

1961:   *Ken, Barbie's boyfriend*

1962:   *Midge, Barbie's best friend*

1964:   *Allen, Midge's boyfriend and Ken's best friend (followed by friends Brad and Curtis)*

1964:   *Skipper, Barbie's little sister*

1965:   *Skooter and "boy next door" Ricky*

1966:   *Francie, mod cousin with real eyelashes and "teen" figure*

1967:   *Twiggy, first celebrity Barbie*

1968:   *Christie, African American friend*

1971:   *Malibu Barbie moves to California*

1977:   *Superstar Barbie gets big hair and Farrah Fawcett smile*

1992:   *Teen Talk Barbie can say "Will we ever have enough clothes?" and "Math class is tough!"*

2004:   *Ken and Barbie break up*

2004:   *Blaine Gordon is Barbie's new Australian boyfriend*

2004:   *Ken is discontinued*

2006:   *NEW Outback Ken comes with open-air Jeep and real working rifle*

2006:   *Blaine goes missing after fishing trip*

2006: *Officer Ken uses Ken's exact body mold but claims not to know Ken*

2007: *Blaine's body found in a dumpster*

2008: *Ken relocates to Chicago and moves in with*

2009: *Totally Stylin' Tattoos Barbie (later recalled)*

2010: *Barbie totals Dream Car*

2011: *Midge is pregnant with removable magnetic baby*

2011: *Ken and Barbie get back together on Valentine's Day*

2015: *Barbie gets adjustable ankles and can wear flat shoes*

2016: *"I Can Be President" Barbie comes in three skin colors*

* * * * *

After the Rapture, Candy Corn brand candy released a statement that said, among other things: "In today's changing world, Candy Corn belongs to another time. We thank you for your many years of patronage."

Within hours there were lines snaking around the corner at every supermarket and drugstore, and by nightfall most regular people, many who didn't even like Candy Corn, were camping out on sidewalks as remaining bags were $14.99, then $29.99, then quickly jumped to $59.99.

Not since the Holland tulip bulb craze of 1637 has anything increased in value so quickly. Once bags of Candy Corn hit $100, market speculation went into overdrive. Day traders and small-time investors began looking for the most exotic, most perfectly shaped corn. Then the big-time investors started trading individual corns on Wall Street, corns that could eventually be worth an entire year's salary. Regular people were borrowing from their IRAs, cashing out their retirement funds, liquidating their savings, and taking out second mortgages with promises of a 40 to 1 return on investment that would fund college tuitions and future dental work and retirement cabanas on tropical beaches. At the peak of the bubble, a man bought an entire island with a single corn.

Then, just as quietly as they'd bought Candy Corn, they began selling. People in the know who still had Candy Corn stashed in their walls or hidden behind loose bricks in the cellar started unloading and fast to glowing and grateful buyers for up to $50,000 a corn, a damn bargain they'd thought until they discovered the market had crashed and their purchases were worthless, leaving them penniless and destitute, full of cavities, forced to eat their investments.

* * * * *

After the Rapture, on a day that would be known in infamy as Black Wednesday, everyone with a credit card got a notice: all balances were now due, in full.

We didn't know you could even do that! the people said. So naturally they went to the banks, but the banks said, You know it doesn't work that way, we don't really have it, and they shut and locked their doors.

* * * * *

Karaoke Gangs Terrorize Kansas City

KANSAS CITY—One man was killed and three more were injured in another gang-related incident at Suki's Chinese restaurant and karaoke bar late Sunday night. Last night's shootout is just the latest in a series of karaoke gang-related activity that has plagued Kansas City strip malls and sports bars since the crisis began. Gang members have been staking out turf such as Suki's and terrorizing the staff and other clients. Turf wars have essentially split the karaoke songbook, and last night's murder was over "Purple Rain."

Tensions still run high in this humble mom and pop restaurant. Owner Suki said she only started karaoke night as a way to bring in weekday business, she had no idea it was going to lead to this.

* * * * *

After the Rapture the people built a wall—those with debt on one side, those without on the other.

It was just easier that way.

* * * * *

After the Rapture, the people needed answers, but there were no answers, so they were turning to the Dark Web, where for a small fee you could purchase a brand-new identity. The people found it comforting to look through the eyes of someone else, to see if the color red was the same color red.

* * * * *

Karaoke Gangs Force
City to Institute Curfew

KANSAS CITY—Karaoke gang activity has continued to spike, and Wednesday night's clash of two of the largest gangs also involved a violent altercation with a karaoke DJ who's still in critical condition.

DJ X, 31, claims violence broke out shortly after he took the microphone away from a gang member trying to sing three times in row, landing X in the hospital with six broken ribs and unforeseen complications to his recent vasectomy.

Duff's Bar and Grill owner Bill (Duff) Dixon says, "We've been doing our best to avoid such incidents and will suspend karaoke night at Duff's until further notice."

Karaoke gangs have been active in all the major cities, but Kansas City will go on lockdown after 8 p.m. through the holidays. People are warned not to venture out unless absolutely necessary.

* * * * *

After the Rapture, but before the Revolution, the people decided they didn't want to feel any more pain—it was too much. But the pain had to go somewhere. The scientists pointed to the artists— that's your job, right?

The artists had never really seen it that way, but they agreed it was probably for the best.

To make it easier, all the artists were gathered together and relocated to the outskirts of town where they bought RVs and tents and set up permanent camps and grew their hair and didn't wash and wore strange clothes and eventually they were only seen in groups at Walmart, restocking supplies.

And they were mostly forgotten. Regular children dared each other to go to the camps but mostly they didn't—too afraid to be snatched and eaten. And everyone forgot they'd been the artists, only knew them now as the weirdos outside of town, and when in the middle of the night their art would be smuggled back into the city the people would marvel at its painful beauty, buy it and hang it on their walls, put it on their bookshelves, but had no idea, really, what it meant. They only knew it tickled something forgotten, something buried so far down it seemed like a past life memory. Like an alternate childhood. Like fear.

* * * * *

Bachelorette Caught in
Karaoke Gang Crossfires

KANSAS CITY—Escalation of karaoke-related turf wars have now included violent run-ins with innocent bystanders. Bachelorette Briana Smith, 22, was visiting O'Malley's with her bridesmaid party when gang members forced her to play karaoke roulette then dragged her into the bathroom where she was later found by medics.

While doctors say Smith will make a full recovery, the wedding has been postponed indefinitely.

* * * * *

Barbie Fun Facts

Full name: Barbara Millicent Roberts
Occupation: "Teen Age Fashion Model"
Parents: George and Margaret Roberts
Hometown: Willows, Wisconsin
Birthday: March 9, 1959
Sign: Pisces
Original hair color: Brunette
Years without smiling: 12
Turn-ons: Yachts, champagne
Turn-offs: Moustaches
National Scandals: Bellybutton Barbie
Presidential runs: 6
Secret fantasy: Crying
Cult of Personality: Yes

* * * * *

After the Rapture, but before the Revolution, angels began to live among us. You could spot them by their outdated haircuts and odd names, the way they were so damn excited about everything, the way they smiled awkwardly from across the room, from across the aisle on the bus, maybe slipped you a sweaty napkin note.

But, because the people were extremely jumpy by now, the angels were also called provocateurs and double agents and told to "go home" (which was where?). And since no one knew who they were, everyone began to suspect everyone, and neighbors tried to spot "angel-like" behavior, and some people claimed to be angels on late night TV, and there were videos of people with flashlights hunting the angels, and there were shocking scenes of suspected angels being strung up by their lack of wings and left to rot at the entrance to backwater towns—No Angels.

＊ ＊ ＊ ＊ ＊

And then The Government announced they were shutting down for good. Good luck making it without us, they said.

We didn't even know you could do that! the people said as they tried to figure out how to change a traffic signal lightbulb.

* * * * *

And then the electricity went out. The hum of the ceiling fan ceased, the time on the stove disappeared, and the electric keyboard stopped playing mid-song.

The people stepped outside to see if it was just them or the whole block. They congregated on porches, and they took their dogs for extra-long walks, and they shut off their phones to save the batteries, and they tested the hot water in the reserve. While the afternoon stretched on they caught up on magazines and visited the neglected pool and went for bike rides and exchanged updates.

By evening they lit grills and cooked all the meat thawing inside the freezers, happy to finally use the patio table. As the sun set, they located matches and flashlights and candles, a novelty for kids who pretended to be pioneers, and families sat outside and remarked how nice this was, really. Some of them stayed up late in the quiet August candlelight having conversations they'd never had, and others went to bed early for once.

But the power never came back on. By morning the neighbors were hand cranking their heavy garages open, and by mid-afternoon the charm and novelty of the whole thing was gone. Most of them headed off to work only to find stoplights were black, frazzled citizens were attempting to hand direct traffic, and most arrived at darkened jobs that couldn't properly function and were home by noon, sniffing the lukewarm milk and checking the remaining charge on their phones.

And this is how it happens: It happens quietly, while people are sniffing milk and looking for batteries. Most people didn't even complain when their passports were eventually taken.

And even after it happened people continued paying their bills for months, like those concentration camp victims who, when the Allied troops came to liberate them, didn't know they were already free.

* * * * *

The first thing the New Government did was offer the citizens a "revolutionary solution," a long-term interest-free solution, the Individual Government Bailout soon to be known as: The Diamond Credit Line.

This deal seemed too sweet to pass up for most, who started using their new Diamond cards without hesitation. The initial credit line was quickly expanded to include bonus incentives: housing incentives for those who purchased a new home, health incentives for those who quit smoking or donated sperm. There were incentives for buying American-made televisions and computers and cars. There were incentives for visiting Disney World and joining the military. There were so many incentives! You could fill out incentive applications on magazine tearaways, the backs of supermarket receipts or internet pop-up screens. The forms were so easy! And it was almost too good to be true— mortgages were paid, refrigerators were replaced, vacations finally taken.

Sometimes you'd see graffiti that said It's All A Lie! But you just ignored that.

* * * * *

Telemarketer Barbie

The Barbie Telemarking Office has realistic pea-green walls and no windows and up to six cubicles for all Barbie's friends!

Skipper, Midge, and even Ken's brother Allen can answer calls in their own cubicles! Comes with script, headphones, and true-to-life fluorescent lighting your child will love. Rapture Hotline, how may I help you?

* * * * *

The Inspectors are coming to the Barbie Dream House. I've never seen them myself but I've heard all the rumors: they're 8 feet tall and tattooed from head to toe, even their tongues. They're all eunuchs, castrated to keep them impartial. They're orphans from birth, all raised in one orphanage in Iowa whose whereabouts are classified.

Regardless if the rumors are true, no one wants the Inspectors coming to their house, even if you are innocent, even if you have nothing to hide.

I've heard stories of the Inspectors coming early on purpose to surprise you, with their clipboards and their lack of humor. So I clean every corner of my house including the crumbs from the Barbie Hummingbird Feeder and then I shower and fuss over what to wear: competent yet effortless, intelligent but also humble, interesting but not too interesting. I pour the milk into a retro glass bottle and put organic stickers on everything and then I floss twice and bake a pie.

When they knock, I let them in—they're large and wear suits that are too tight, like pro-football players in Sunday church clothes. I show them around and they write on their clipboards and I'm glad I organized the Barbie Tupperware drawer because they look.

Back in the living room, they ask me a series of standard questions, including who I'd voted for in the last election and who is my favorite character on *Game of Thrones*. Finally, one says, Is there anything else you'd like to share?

What he means is, are you hiding anything? the other says.

I don't have cable, I confess. I rent *Game of Thrones* and I'm still on season one.

They write it down. Anything else?

I still have the iPhone 4, I say quietly.

They write it down.

And I don't like *Wheel of Fortune*.

Nobody likes *Wheel of Fortune*. What else?

That's it.

Okay. They both write on their clipboards.

Then one holds up a scorecard: 7.2

The other nods, holds up his scorecard: 8.6

Did I pass?

Barely, says 7.2. We'll be watching you.

I show them to the door, where 8.6 slips a business card into my hand—*Call me?* he mouths with a wink.

* * * * *

The Diamond Credit Line

She's your perfect diamond. And she trusts you to provide for her. Now you can.

Let your joyous day be joyous for her, too. Ask your hospital staff to open a Diamond line of credit for your newest diamond today, the only interest-free, government-issued and guaranteed credit account.

*This special introductory offer is for newborns only. Regular application fee is $500 added to your first month's statement.

TERMS AND CONDITIONS

- *By accepting this line of credit you are agreeing to pay the balance each month or*

- *If you do not pay your balance in full, you can choose to have it automatically deducted from your official government paycheck or*

- *If you do not currently have a government job, you will be assigned one.*

- *If you are under 18, your Diamond card repayment will enjoy a grace period until you are 18, at which point you can pay the balance in full or you will be assigned a government position.*

- *Account holders who are under 18 must have an adult beneficiary on the Diamond card account.*

- *In case of natural death, the balance will be passed on to the designated next of kin.*

- *If no next of kin is designated the Diamond Corp. will designate a familial beneficiary for the balance.*

- *In case of suicide the full balance will be passed on to the designated next of kin or assigned beneficiary plus penalties.*

- *After 1 year of official government work and no penalties, you may apply for the Forgiveness Track.*

- *If accepted onto the Forgiveness Track, your balance will be forgiven in full after 50 years of work at an official government job with no penalties.*

- *To be considered for the Forgiveness Track you must apply in writing. Please list job skills, work experience, and attach a current CV or resume. If you have no work experience, a position will be assigned to you. If there is a particular position you feel most suited for please include a 1,000-word essay outlining your background and why you are uniquely qualified for the position.*

- *At any point during the Forgiveness Track you may designate an able-bodied next of kin to finish the repayment or merge the balance with a previously active balance.*

- *If for any reason your government position is terminated by either employer or employee, the Diamond card balance will be due in full.*

HELPFUL NUMBERS
24-hour customer service: 888-888-8888
Suicide hotline: 666-666-6666

* * * * *

After the Rapture, the people tried to sue religion. You told us we would be spared—that we would be lifted out of this mess! But we're still here!

The religious leaders had no response, for they, too, were still here. No one had been spared.

So the religious leaders locked themselves in a heavily guarded suite on the top floor of a Marriott and there they stayed for many days while the whole world speculated. And when they didn't emerge after a week, the people started marching and holding signs that said things like Not My Rapture! or Liars Burn in Eternal Hellfire! And if you'd been on a balcony or could sit on someone's shoulders you would have seen a savannah of people all the way to the horizon and an electrical charge hanging in the balance like a baby going from laughing to crying to laughing again.

And when the religious leaders *still* hadn't emerged, someone yelled that we shouldn't listen to the religious leaders anyway—they were all just phonies who'd led us astray! We don't need their god...we can make our own god! And then the disgruntled started rocking parked cars and shouting obscenities from the branches of trees while everyone else started chanting: Make a God! Make a God! And then uniformed men on horses came and shot rubber bullets at the crowd and told everyone to disperse, and some people asked what crime they were committing, but that was the wrong question because then there was tear gas, rolling across the asphalt like spinning firecrackers shooting orange smoke, and all you could do was run and try not to get trampled while the chemicals creeped into your mouth and nostrils, stinging your eyes until you couldn't see anything and you were gagging and horses were clopping and the people were coughing and gasping for air and that's when you began to hate.

Finally, amidst the chaos in the streets, the religious leaders held a highly publicized press conference from their hotel room at the top of the Marriott and issued this statement: "After much time deliberating, we have unanimously decided that the failure of the Rapture to either end the world or spare any of its faithful servants is because what we have called the Rapture was not the real end of the world but only a false rapture manufactured by the false prophet. This Antichrist has clearly arrived and was sent to Earth as a final test of the faithful. We must all stay vigilant for the real end of the world. Thank you and God bless."

* * * * *

BREAKING NEWS—We're coming to you live from the Marriott lawn. Wow, what an announcement! So the big question on everyone's mind now is: Who is the Antichrist? Jim, what do you think?

Well, there are several strong contenders of course, but I think he's probably been right under our radar all this time.

Incredible.

Yes, and Political #6 is looking like the guy to beat right now. He doesn't appear remorseful or to have aged in the last several decades.

Oh yes, it's almost too obvious.

Exactly. Which is why it could be a ploy to distract us from Religious Leader #3.

Yes, and what a story: He came from the streets of Big City where he became an asshole at a young age to survive.

Agreed. But there is one more serious contender at this point, CEO #5, a real heart-tugger story.

Right. At one point he actually fell in love and almost went straight!

Truly incredible...And that's all the time we have, folks! Remember to drink Fun! The fizzy, citrusy goodness of Fun! will keep your days as sunny and sweet as the first day of summer every day of the year.

* * * * *

Hundreds Storm Hotel in the
Wake of Rapture Talks

MARRIOTT, USA—In the middle of a riot between police and protesters, as many as 150 protesters stormed a local Marriott hotel late last night and are refusing to come out. The military has surrounded the hotel, but people in communication with those on the inside say they will stay until their demands are met.

"They promised us a rapture, now give us a rapture," said one man on the street. "Those people in there are heroes."

But not everyone thinks they're heroes. Said one soldier: "When they come out, we'll arrest them and take them to jail where criminals belong."

While the religious leaders were lifted to safety in helicopters at the first sign of clashes, it's estimated there are between 100-150 people inside the hotel and as many as 25 staff members. Experts predict there is enough food inside the Marriott to last five days if properly rationed.

"They have plenty of food," say police. "Let's not turn these people into martyrs."

Religious leaders converged at the Marriott just one week ago to discuss what is now being called the "rapture problem." Protesters and police have been engaged in hostilities since the official press release yesterday.

"We were promised a rapture," said one protester. "These leaders owe us."

Our thoughts and prayers are with the families.

Stay tuned to this station for 24-hour coverage of the Rapture Standoff.

* * * * *

EMERGENCY NOTICE—We interrupt this program to bring you this breaking news: Scientists say that due to elevated sonar frequencies in the atmosphere, the Antichrist may already be among us. We take you now to head scientist Dr. Z, reporting live from Important University. Dr. Z, what can you tell us about the Antichrist?

Dr. Z: Well, what we know for certain is that the Antichrist will be horribly frightening, more frightening than humanity can even imagine.

What can our listeners be on the lookout for?

Dr. Z: Everyone should be on the lookout for anyone who is a little odd or unusual. Maybe they don't mow their lawn or maybe they watch too many foreign movies, that sort of thing.

Oh wow. I have several neighbors in mind already.

Dr. Z: Yes. The Antichrist may also have what they used to call the witch's teat—a mysterious growth through which the devil communicates directly. This teat can be anywhere on the body including under the hair, so those working in barber shops and salons should be especially vigilant.

Good advice. Is there anything else our listeners can do to keep their loved ones safe?

Dr. Z: Remember if you see a suspicious person, do not confront or try to contain them on your own. Contact the proper authorities immediately and consider the individual to be extremely dangerous.

Thank you for your time, Dr. Z. And to our listeners, you can contact the station directly or call 911. We now return you to your story already in progress:

* * * * *

I'm pretty sure the Barbie Dream Landline Phone is tapped. When I pick up the receiver there they are, breathing or chewing on the other end. At first, it was kind of cool, like in the old movies. I'd be in the middle of a conversation and then both of us would hear clicking or a weird echo:

What was that?

I think your phone is tapped, Ken said.

The people tapping my phone aren't subtle. Sometimes I'll pick up the phone and there will be no dial tone at all, just the generic sounds of an office in the background, papers rustling, indiscriminate machines. Like they've stepped away from spying to get a drink of water or a smoke and I'm forced to wait for them to return and give me my dial tone.

No one believes me. So I've stopped paying my bill and figure when they shut off my phone that will be the end of it.

> We interrupt this program to bring you an urgent update. The nation is now on High Alert. We have no further information at this time but will keep you updated. We now return you to your story in progress:

But they never shut off my phone. The office sounds continue, and next month's bill has a $200 credit.

I call the Phone Company. I'd like to cancel my service, I say.

No problem, she says to the sounds of typing. Let me pull up your account.

Oh, that's strange, she says. Let me put you on hold.

And then the phone goes dead.

* * * * *

I'm at Water World when I hear the announcement: *Good afternoon, Water World guests. We have an important call waiting for a guest by the name of*—and she says my name—*Please come to any guest services.*

The kiosk is staffed by teenagers. I have a message?

A kid hands me an actual red phone:

Hello?

Congratulations! You've just been chosen to star on our Water World reality show, *Escape from Water World*! The way the game works is you have 60 minutes to find the key to your locker and leave the park. If you don't find the key in time, the contents of your locker will be forfeited.

But my purse and my Diamond card and keys are in there.

Yes! And you have 60 minutes to find them and—here a studio audience chimes in—*Escape! From! Water! World!* There's cheering in the background. Are you ready for your first clue?

I don't want to play this game, actually—

Don't hang up—we're already filming.

The guest services kid gives me a thumbs-up.

Your first clue is: The woman in the pink has gotten too much sun. Find her and find Clue #1. And...begin! Sixty minutes on the clock starting now!

This is ridiculous! I yell but he's already gone. I hang up and walk straight to my locker, where the wristband key no longer works, buzzing angry with each failed try.

A teenager in the raft rental booth yells, You can do it!

There are probably 5,000 people at Water World. There is absolutely no way I'm going to play this stupid game. I need to

find an adult employee, any adult at all. I approach an old man
sweeping up around the picnic areas.

Excuse me, can you help me?

He smiles knowingly. If you want a clue to the pink woman,
she *might* be on the Ancient Journey to the Pharaoh's ride.

That's not the kind of help I want!

The concrete is atomic hot as I hop from patch of shade to
patch of shade. People on beach loungers grin and whisper and
give me the thumbs up, past the Dip-n-Dots and the deep-fried
Twinkie sundae funnel cake booth, past the wave pool in motion,
where a kid on an inflatable shark yells, I believe in you! and
onto the AstroTurf beach toward the Pharaoh's ride.

Now I'm in line with all the wet people and their bad tattoos—
the US Constitution inked across a chest, a portrait of Walter
Cronkite distorted into cleavage, actual "guns" tattooed on both
biceps—and at the front of the line I'm put into a raft with a family
who needs a single rider.

The ride heads into a pyramid. The mom asks: Any luck?

What?

You *know*, she winks. She has a terrible sunburn all over her
body. The family all looks like they're about to burst.

Are you the "pink" lady?

Your last clue is this, she says, cutting me off: The man with
the gospel on his back will show you where the key is at!

This is so fucked up, I yell as the kids blush, and as soon as the
ride is over I stomp across hot concrete back to the guest services
kiosk and yell at the kid—who's a different kid now:

Look. I don't want to play this game! Just open my locker!

He looks sympathetic and hands me the phone again:

Ooh! A buzzer sounds loudly in my ear. Darn! says the voice. You didn't beat the clock. Well, you're still going home with some nice parting gifts. Jonny, can you tell us what they are?

I hang up. The kid hands me a red bag with *Escape from Water World* written on the side. Inside are tubes of sunscreen, a bright green sun visor and a sippy bottle with the Water World logo.

You also have salmonella, he says.

I walk back to my towel and my locker door is standing open, locker empty.

* * * * *

And then I get a call from a blocked number—We've recovered your arm! they say, perhaps a little too enthusiastically. But you'll need to come down to the station and identify it.

Ken can't believe it either. Wow, that's incredible, he says. So... what happens with us, then?

What do you mean?

You know, he gestures. Are we still good?

Probably a bunch of drug addicts, the lady shouts as we drive a little golf cart to the reclaiming room. Drug addicts will steal a body part, use it for a while and then abandon it. We recovered it from underneath the viaduct where the old rubber factory was. I should warn you: it looks pretty rough.

She leads me to a corner where something is wrapped in a tarp. It doesn't look too bad from this angle but underneath— she rolls it over slightly and I cover my nose. My arm—if you could call it that—is greenish and covered in white cheese like a stillborn baby.

Are you sure that's my arm?

Do you want it or not?

I'm not sure it *is* an arm.

We're going to need a DNA test from you either way.

Why?

It's standard. She looks away. I see you already got a replacement.

This is a Barbie arm.

If you say so.

I watch her load the arm onto a conveyor belt bound for the dump and I touch it one last time, remembering the feeling of my own skin, now cold and weird. Like tragedy.

* * * * *

The Barbie Dream Car

Get away from it all in the new Barbie brand convertible Dream Car! Your child will love driving Barbie along the coast with the top down, wind sweeping her long, gorgeous real hair! Barbie comes with sunglasses and head scarf to blow in the breeze!

The all-new Barbie Dream Car has faux leather interior, a steering wheel that turns, and a real working horn! Out of the way, protesters! Passenger seat can hold any of Barbie's friends and the odometer tells your child how far you've driven. Not far enough, says Barbie! [*Goes well with the Barbie Motel, sold separately.*]

* * * * *

The Barbie Motel

After a long day of driving, Barbie is tired and ready to rest her head at the Barbie brand motel! The Barbie Motel comes with vintage neon that turns on and off and a real vacancy/no vacancy sign that your child will love! Look who's working the Registration Desk? It's Ken! What are you doing here, Ken? I just wanted to talk, says Ken. He's followed Barbie. He's sorry but Barbie says no chance! Good for you, Barbie!

Barbie comes with charge cards, suitcase, wig and dark sunglasses. Barbie Motel has empty swimming pool, ice machine that makes real ice [*not suitable for human consumption*], and a telephone. What's that? Ken has cut the line? Never fear, Barbie always finds a way! [*Pairs well with Barbie Telephone Booth, sold separately.*]

Part Three

The camp is built around tents, clotheslines, dogs. What happened to your arm? she asks.

Long story.

Fucking Babylon, she says. You'll be safe here. How are things down there?

Worse than ever.

Not surprised.

It's like they don't even care.

They don't care, she says. They can't care, it would kill them.

We walk through the camp. Most people sit quietly smoking. Someone strums a guitar. Dogs loot through trash. Want a cigarette, she asks? It helps with the despair.

I take one for later. Didn't you used to be the artists?

We're still the artists.

But when do you make the art?

We're always making art. Look. She bends a tree branch. Art.

But how is this helping?

I don't know if it's helping anymore, she says.

* * * * *

Rapture Hotline: How may I help you?

I'd like to report a possible Antichrist sighting.

Where are you?

I'm at Red Lobster.

Why are you whispering?

I think he might be a couple of tables away.

You're sure?

Pretty sure—he has a big Tom Selleck mustache and his date is smoking a cigar.

Anything else suspicious?

The whole thing is suspicious, really. Actually, I think it might be Tom Selleck—they just ordered oysters—I'm by the bathrooms so I'm not sure.

Okay, we'll send someone out. Thanks for the tip!

* * * * *

And then they gave us the official "Countdown to the Antichrist" and issued their final warning. They called it the Event of the Century! which was good since the Rapture had been such a bust. You could see it in their eyes, how badly they needed this.

* * * * *

And then an emergency signal was created and people got very loud test alerts and a stage was built with capacity for the Largest Audience Possible and Las Vegas bookies were taking bets and you could *Prepare for the Antichrist with Pepsi!* and every newspaper claimed to know who it was and they had alternate front pages printed and alternate t-shirts printed and it never occurred to anyone that one day those shirts would end up halfway around the world, worn by children who didn't give a shit about any of this.

* * * * *

And there were rumors of resistance camps hidden in the hills, and regular people were too scared to be helpful, now, terrified to be turned in for being an angel or a sympathizer or worse, and groups of heavy, official-sounding boots shuffled each night through the streets while the people smoked behind locked doors and away from windows and their faces became deeply lined, their hair prematurely gray. Families kept sleeping bags in the living room and slept with all their clothes and shoes on, just in case, because everyone remembered what had happened before. They remembered when one of theirs had been dragged off: the pounding at the door, the flashlights, the boots, that last look in the eye as you said an abrupt goodbye.

✳ ✳ ✳ ✳ ✳

Checkpoint Barbie

You want to get through? We'll need to see your papers!

Your child will love detaining Barbie and her friends at this true-to-life security checkpoint, complete with barbed witnesses, armed gurus, and real guns! Ken, what the hell are you doing? Barbie says while he dumps her purse in the dirt. We need names, Ken says. Who have you seen, who have you talked to? Leave Barbie in the hot sun while Ken makes imaginary phone calls! Extra paperwork included!

You can go, Ken finally says.

That was close, Barbie!

* * * * *

The Rapture Madness began when two kids in an elementary school sandbox started itching for no reason and their tongues became inflamed and their eyes streamed with tears: It burns! they cried, running to the sinks. It burns! they screamed and drooled and water didn't help and some of the teachers went to the sandbox, and their eyes and noses and mouths also started burning and the hazmat team came and set up sterile tunnels of plastic from room to room and all the parents got emergency notifications and the school was surrounded and there were panicked whispers of chemical warfare, and camera crews were reporting live, and students were processed through a strip search and a neutralizing chemical power wash and some kids were left with black eyes from the whole ordeal and everyone got really, really mad.

And the gurus re-emerged, and there were many, many instructions on how to be properly mad, and some people got mad at the gurus because they could only be mad a certain way, and some people got mad at other people for not being mad at the correct thing, or in the correct manner, and sometimes we weren't sure which was worse, the original thing we were mad about or the people who weren't mad enough about that thing.

And then someone decided we should all go outside and scream, all at the same time, to show how mad we really were, and that seemed like a great idea, so we all went outside and we screamed and we shook our fists in the air and recorded ourselves shaking our fists, and some people remembered the Bad Thing from so long ago—oh, how naïve we'd been! Oh, how we longed for those early days of colors and hope! And we painted our doorways with the sacrificial blood of whatever we could find, and there were mass circumcisions, just in case, and libraries were torched, and Fun! changed its name to Extreme Fun! and the dictator became a portrait painter and regular people were turning into pillars of salt and the men from Mars were eating cars, and eating bars, and there was dried blood everywhere.

And still the madness bulged and swelled. We gave it to our lovers. We gave it to our children. The madness itched and burned. There were creams and ointments. We were told to stay inside—the madness was out there. The madness was on our walls. We ate the madness and took pictures of ourselves eating it. We wiped the madness on our faces and on our arms and legs. The madness smelled like lavender. The madness smelled like garbage. We hated the madness. We loved it.

They say you can tell a lot about a person by the way they go over the edge; some people went singing and some screamed like children and others went in absolute silence.

* * * * *

Every day I spend at the camp there are changes: Something turns pink here. Something stiffens and becomes plastic there. I wait, watching the light break in the morning, glide across the sky all afternoon, dissipate into the night.

How long will I have to wait?

You'll know, they say. It's different for everyone.

It was almost three weeks before I felt the first little rock, a hard, foreign object resting just under the surface of my skin. I could move it gently with my fingers, and as I touched it, I began to remember things I'd forgotten: After the windshield shattered and sprayed my body with glass like a glittering piñata, after they ripped the doors off and broke out the remaining windows, after they pressed masking tape on my glittering eyelashes and wiped glass dust out of my nose and mouth, after I spat glass and they pushed brushes as deep into the gashes as they dared...

They say after an accident, the body will naturally expel any remaining glass over time (bodies are interesting like that). The hard rock grew more insistent, rising to the surface like strange sweat. One day, a sharp edge poked through the skin. I caressed the pointed tip, marveled at the way it sparkled in the sunlight, piercing itself free from my flesh. The day it fully emerged, it was shaped like a tear.

* * * * *

The second angel appears at my bed carrying a harp. Would you like some music? she asks. She settles herself on a portable stool, rearranging her sheet music. Her finger placements are tentative, plucking awkward. I just learned to play, she admits as I cry.

* * * * *

Ready for the Rapture Barbie

A new era deserves a new Barbie!

Meet Rapture Barbie, the woman who's ready for the Rapture and more. Your child will love the realistic gasmask and fireproof poncho! Rapture Barbie comes with canned rations, Barbie Mess Kit, bulletproof vest and emergency cell phone for all those crazy mishaps. Someone trapped in the hotel after curfew? No problem! Barbie will save the day in her real working flak jacket! Rubber bullets in the crowd? No problem! Barbie is a certified medic who comes with first aid kit including iodine, splint, and onions in a baggie to neutralize tear gas! What's that? Barbie's making a call to the embassy? Evacuation? No chance! they say. Barbie tells them to @%$^* themselves!! Way to tell them off, Barbie! Wait, why are you crying? Comes with passport, high-powered flashlight, white flag and permanent magic marker to write your blood type on your arm—Barbie is A+. Skipper is the universal donor! Ken, get away from that window, don't you know there are snipers? Oh, look, Dan Rather Barbie has just shown up in a news van with his camera crew! Barbie's going to be on television! [*Dan Rather Barbie and blood testing kit sold separately.*]

* * * * *

It's time. They tell me I'm ready. It's comforting to pretend none of this is happening, but I know I have to go back. It's gonna seem really weird, they warn me. It was weird before I got here, I say. It's gonna be weirder, they say. Brace yourself.

And they hand me a white flag.

* * * * *

We walk to the edge of the camp and they point the way. Dogs are barking. Roosters crow in the middle of the day. Gunshots in the distance, booming, *rat-a-tat-tat*. The sky is thick, oatmeal flakes. Roads are littered with empty bullet casings, a telephone booth flattened like a soda can. Buildings caved in and others sliced open like a three-layer birthday cake.

Now I run. Weird fireworks in the distance; street signs and billboards polka-dotted with charred black rings; television set bombs wired across an empty road; a pockmarked wall, possible snipers taking aim between my shoulder blades; a convoy of pink tanks and APCs and when the smoke clears, the truth spreads out before me as if a bottle of Pepto Bismol has exploded—

> *We interrupt this program to bring you urgent news. According to inside sources, the Antichrist has officially been spotted. We repeat: The Antichrist has been spotted. While we have no further information at this time, we will keep you updated. We now return you to your story in progress:*

—over the Barbie Drive-in Theater, the Barbie Dream Wedding Shopping Plaza, the Barbie Organic Food Mart, the Barbie Dive Bar, the Barbie Vintage Thrift Store, Barbie Liquor Store, Barbie FDIC Insured Bank, and the Barbie High Security Prison—what had been not-pink was now pink: pink buildings, pink carwashes with happy people washing pink streets, pink sky, pink clouds, pink sadness pink money pink Walmart with pink guard dogs and pink watchtowers pink cops and pink cobblestones streets where they walk with pink smiles, pink frustration pink gall bladder pink retirement, pink abortion pink embarrassment pink oxygen tank pink sunset over pink dumpsters pink government housing, pink colonoscopy with happy pink peppermint streetwalkers, pink skylight, pink sadness pink abrasives pink mongrel; the Barbie groom storefront and the Barbie pinnacle abrasions—the Barbie muckraker theater and the Barbie aphrodisiac hubcap, Barbie groundswell and Barbie apologia huckster and the Barbie Babylonian boudoir—pin-up mongoose barbed wisdom punk pin-up back highway hijack pin-up streetcar skydiver, pin-up cloudbursts, pin-up sadness pin-up abortionists pin-up moneylender pin-up wasteland with guardian dogcarts and pin-up cockfight stretcher-bearers and pin-up streetwalker cobras on permanent tirade, pin-up blasphemy retort, pin-up embassy pin-up pachyderm hovel, pin-up gradient hubcap, pin-up schoolmistress pin-up hairpiece pin-up interstate hillbilly with Madonna and chimera.

I'm out of breath by the time I make it back to what's left of the Barbie Dream House, a pyramid of pink pizza boxes, cigarette butts, glassy-eyed squatters. They're staring at me suspiciously, and I see it in their eyes even before I look in the mirror: Now, instead of having a Barbie arm, I have a real human arm. But the rest? I touch my face with my long-forgotten hand, but I already know what I'm going to find.

Hello beautiful, says Ken. Welcome home.

* * * * *

And then, my faithful congregation, we arrived in an erosion of umbrellas! Look around, my fripperies, the Great Trick is upon us! Some of you might even cry: Isn't there supposed to be chagrin in fame? Well they wouldn't call it fame if it was easy! If there was a monogramed backwater guillotine, then everyone would be here! We don't get thirty deacons to try out fame and return it if threesomes don't happen the week we planned! No, my friends, the great go-getter has told us to wait for a signature. In fallacy. Together. And we wait because we know that the fake will be harvested from the falsetto like the wheat from the chaff. The announcers said, Fallen, fallen is Babylon the great, she who has made all the navels drizzle of the pastry of her advertisers. Yes, my friends, the advertisers are already among us, and they will reverse the beckon of Babylon in due time.

Now open your hymnals and turn to number #382 and let us continue to ramrod our voluntaries in sorrow: *After the Rapture, more Bad Things happened...*

* * * * *

And the people said, *it can never get worse than this!* and they dug out all the old colors, and the old bracelets, and rival countries decided to come together and make a solid plan, so they brought back the scientists, who thought we should transport all the icebergs into all the deserts, which seemed like a terrible plan, but no one had a better one, so everyone got to work devising ways to lift massive icebergs and transport them thousands of miles mostly intact. They only managed to do it with one, though, and considering the cost it took in both money and lives, that was probably enough.

* * * * *

And with each passing day, that which had been outlandish was no longer outlandish, that which had been metaphor was now truth, and the people watched the edge disappear like a baby slowly being crushed, like a ridiculous auto-da-fé, and that slow burn was perhaps the worst of all.

* * * * *

Barbie and Frills Marx Labyrinth!

The Barbie Marx Labyrinth features Beebop Barbie and her sidetrack Skittle, who come with adorable dashboard glimpses, piranha pirates, and a firebrick extrapolation for all those crazy mispronunciations! Comes with dry ideals for special effusions! [*Please do not let your child use dry ideology without proper supplication.*]

＊ ＊ ＊ ＊ ＊

And then I get a cryptic message: I have something you want, he says. You pick the place and I'll be there.

Do I know you?

No, but I know you. Meet me at the Barbie Nightclub in one hour. It's Ladies Night, he adds. So you get in free.

The Barbie Nightclub smells like sweat and pomade and plastic. Everyone is smiling and no one is blinking.

This is a strange place to meet, I shout.

I thought you would be taller, he shouts back. You want a drink or something?

No, I'm okay. What's this about?

I'm ready to make a deal.

What? I shout.

I'm ready to *make a deal*, if you know what I mean.

No, I don't.

That's great, of course you don't, he says, winking. Can't be too careful, right?

Do you want to go outside? It's so noisy in here.

Yeah, great idea.

We go outside and he asks for a cigarette from the sweaty group smoking—Sorry, nervous, he says. You don't mind, right— of course you don't. He lights it with a borrowed lighter.

Look, you better tell me what's going on.

You're right, he says, exhaling a sigh of smoke. The cigarette's half gone already. We step away where it's quieter. Okay, so I'm just going to lay it out there, he says. Whew, I can't believe I'm going to do this.

Just do it, I say, getting impatient.

Ok, here goes, he says. So, I've been a musician since I was five. A good one, too. Everyone said I had talent—I *have* talent. And I know it's my own fault, I missed the boat when I was young, long story: car accident, thought there was plenty of time, etc. But now I'm realizing there isn't much time. I thought I would've won a Grammy by now. I thought I'd be traveling the world on private jets to play in Europe and stuff and, well, I've been telling myself it was okay, I'd let it go gracefully, but then I see all these young musicians winning all these awards, and I'm pissed.

Well, that's understandable.

Thank you, he stammers, then gaining confidence. Yes, *thank you*, dammit. I know it's mostly luck and age and who you know and all that BS, and I know not everyone gets to win a Grammy, but—and here he looks at me directly for the first time—I'm ready.

For what?

To win a Grammy! To make a deal!

Well, that's great, I'm sure you can do it, I say, trying to be encouraging.

So...let's do this.

Do what?

You know. *The deal.*

I'm sorry, but I have no idea what you're talking about.

He narrows his eyes. Is this part of the test? How bad I want it and stuff?

No, really. I'm serious.

Whew, okay, good, because I'm nervous enough, he says. I didn't even tell my girlfriend.

We're both silent while he continues to suck on the butt of the dead cigarette. Finally, I say, Well, I think I'm gonna go but good luck?

Is that it? he says. Don't you want me to sign something? I mean...am I good? Do I just go home?

Look, I don't know who you think I am—

Aren't you—? He says my name.

Yes. But maybe you've mistaken me for someone else—

No, he says. You're the one that's been all over the news. The one everyone's been talking about. He points to my arm: You're the devil. The Antichrist.

* * * * *

RECALL NOTICE: The Safe Drinking Water and Toxic Enforcement Act requires mandatory toxic content reporting from manufacturers to disclose substances known to cause cancer, birth defects, and reproductive harm. In compliance with the Safe Drinking Water and Toxic Enforcement Act, it has been reported that the following item or items may be contaminated with toxic levels of one or more substances:

Barbie Dream House
Barbie Sperm Bank
I Can Shower Barbie
Barbie and Friends Go-Go Club
Bachelor Party Ken
Evangelical Barbie
World War II Barbie
Barbie and Friends Organ Donation
Barbie Food Stamp Office
Barbie and Friends Neonatal Intensive Care Unit
Werner Hertzog Barbie

WARNING: If you feel yourself becoming dizzy or experience a localized rash please see your health care practitioner immediately. By purchasing this product you are waiving any responsibility, liability or health complications that may occur.

* * * * *

Rapture Hotline. How may I help you?

This has got to stop!

Please stay on the line while I patch you through, she says.

My missing person poster now has devil horns and a goatee and a forked tail and a crude Barbie arm with the middle finger up and everything smells like burned plastic and fear.

Why is this poster still here! I already told you I'm not missing!

May I put you on a brief hold? And she's replaced by the sounds of Hall and Oates. *Watch out boy she'll chew you up.*

Thank you for waiting. I have my manager here.

Hello, Miss, how are you doing today?

Not good.

Oh, I'm sorry to hear that, he says. Keep talking so we don't lose contact: Do you feel like you aren't yourself?

Yes.

Like everyone is out to get you?

Yes.

Like no one understands you?

Yes.

Like you were put here for a reason?

Sirens getting louder.

Wait a minute—

Like you're here to save us?

Wait, no.

Do you have any strange marks on your body?

No! What is wrong with you people?!

Please stay on the line so we don't lose contact, he says while a carnival of red and blue lights explodes. Two then three then six cars pull into the parking lot, and men with walkie talkies take positions as a swarm of pink helicopters hover like cotton candy clouds.

Drop the phone!

Ma'am, we're going to need to you come with us, one of them says, approaching slowly.

Ken?

Officer Ken. Brand new. Comes with flashlight. He aims the flashlight in my face. Now put your purse on the ground and keep your hands out of your pockets!

But just as he tries to grab me, 10,000 angels blowing Barbie brand trumpets descend from the clouds:

The wait is over! The time of final judgement is now!

* * * * *

And then all the buildings go up in hot pink flames, and the Four Horsemen gallop by on pink ponies, and the Barbie Archangel fights the Plastic Dragon, and angry pink smoke billows into the darkness, and all around me people rise like fireflies from a field at dusk, tiny motes of light rising, glorious, suspended in a marmalade sky.

The last thing I see is Ken's confused face as I rise into the clouds and *poof!* disappear.

Part Four

The Real Rapture came without preamble. First the moon turned red like a gorgeous, ripe September peach hanging in the sky, a three-dimensional orb you could reach out and pluck right off a black velvet background.

Then the solar flares that were supposedly too far away to hurt us reached Earth, and fiery whips shot from the sun without warning, leaving smoking char lines across the planet like a strange space Zorro. And then the asteroid belt went askew, and asteroids pummeled the Earth's land and sea, and this caused the ocean water to rise and spill into all the sinkholes and douse all the volcanoes and most of the cities were lost.

But sometimes, in those final hours, a solar flare smacked the ocean just so, and such amazing arcs of steam and rainbows sprayed that those left treading water would *ooh* and *ahh* at the strange beauty of this finale, so bittersweet, so different than they'd imagined. It bubbled up and over like drowning, like that first full breath underwater, and in those last moments before they sank to the bottom, the people watched cosmic fires dance with a swirling sea and were struck by how beautiful it had all been, really.

* * * * *

And then, those of us left decided to walk.

We walked west for many days towards the setting sun. We passed the old roadside altars, the faded scraps of fabric tied to a tree. The perfect 4x6 bald spot where no grass will grow. How silly it all seemed, now.

We walked until we reached the edge, a floating monstrosity of nonsense, a multicolored tundra undulating, undulating, and there we tossed the rest of our melancholy dreams and heartsick imaginations and some people even ripped off their tattoos and threw the inked bologna skins over the edge and together we watched them bob and float away like deflated balloons and sad water bugs.

* * * * *

And then the people remembered another dream. A slow dream. A dirty dream. A hallucination dream. They remembered a sweat lodge dream, a pink sky dream. A dream hyperventilating under a bush, a dream that ripped through nylon. A precarious dream, a dream sleeping off the highway back when they were unafraid dream. A dream of reckoning, of prophecy. A dream that birthed another dream, opening like an orchid to the other alone in a tent in the middle of the woods. A dream pretending to be someone else's dream.

And the people remembered the forgetting. The way one forgets so slowly it's almost like not forgetting. But now they remembered the forgetting, the bewilderment, the dream becoming wild in the desert, the deserting, the dream becoming sand, mummified, roped off like a dead child's bedroom. Roped off and forgotten.

We all felt it leaving us. We knew the exact moment it left, a flock of birds flying from an open chest cavity, a turn to the left instead of the right. We watched it float away. As if it never meant anything to anyone.

✶ ✶ ✶ ✶ ✶

And then, just when we thought it was too late, someone jumped in and started swimming. Stunned, we watched them swim far out to a big dream bobbing away, almost lost. And drag it back.

The water lapped our toes like needy children and the silence stretched. We saw dreams littered and broken everywhere, a dumpster caught in trees, a coyote wrapped in barbed wire. We saw the sun, a reluctant prophet in a wallflower sky. We watched the dream and swimmer get bigger, bigger, splitting the water like a muskrat until they finally breeched into a raft of waiting hands, an inhale that passed from person to person.

And then we all jumped in and started swimming.

The dreams were tired but alive. They were trapped in tides and entangled with rocks and some were nearly gone but we rescued them all: the big dreams, the forgotten dreams, the tiny bits of purple dream. Even children were scooping up a floating dream, releasing a dream from under a rock. So many dreams! They were waterlogged and distorted; they were bloated and torn and trampled. But they were alive. We pulled them all out, wet but alive, and piled them on the beach.

And then we ran, bounding across the sand and rocks, arms thrown open like a hundred estranged sons towards a hundred prodigal mothers. We felt ourselves dissolve into a million stars.

* * * * *

And then we decided to give all the dreams back. Each night we returned the dreams, and each morning when the sun rose, ripping pink stretchmarks into the sky, ripping like it had never wanted anything more, the people found their dreams in the door jambs or in the mailboxes or under rocks, returned like love notes, like a lost pet now found, and they wondered how they'd ever let them go so easily.

THE END

Publication Acknowledgements

Excerpts from this manuscript have been published under the following names:

- "The Bad Thing" published by *Connotation Press* and republished in *The Best Small Fictions 2019*
- "Missing" published in *Jellyfish Review*
- "Which World Dictator are You Related To? A Quiz" published by *Flash Boulevard*
- "The Last Orgy" published by *Lost Balloon*
- "The Rapture" published by *Open Arts Journal*
- "Naked" published in *100 Word Story* and reprinted in the anthology *Nothing Short Of: Selected Tales from 100 Word Story*
- "Barbie Arm" published by *bOINK Magazine*
- "The Pilgrimage" published by *La.Lit* and republished in the Flash Frontier Anthology *Ripening*
- "Tiny House" published by *New Flash Fiction Review*
- "Loch Ness" published in *Flash Fiction Festival Vol. Two*
- "The Awakening" published by *Digging Through the Fat Press* and Editor's Choice for Fiction of the Year 2018
- "Courtesy Call" published in *Fiction Kitchen Berlin*
- "Heart of Glass" published by *Flash Fiction Festival Vol. Three*

- "Barbie Motel" published by *Blink Ink* and nominated for a Pushcart Prize
- "Xanadu: a triptych" published in *Matter Press Journal of Compressed Arts*

Author's Note

I wrote this book between 2016 and early 2020, finishing it the same week the world went into quarantine. For the next year I watched the line between truth and satire begin to merge, and in the continuing aftermath it is now impossible to separate the two.

I'm grateful to everyone at Mason Jar Press for their visionary scope and their careful and committed handling of this story.

I'm indebted to my early readers Sally Reno, Jonathan Montgomery, Rob Geisen, James Thomas, Bryan Jansing, and Moria Woodruff. In addition, many of these pieces were performed or published under different titles, so thank you to all the journals, anthologies, editors and audiences who allowed me an early space to find my direction.

I'm incredibly lucky to have family and friends who encourage, support, and inspire me after so many years, especially Nick Busheff, who is more than a creative partner, more than a companion, always.

Other Titles From Mason Jar Press

lesser american boys
short stories by Zach VandeZande

JERKS
short stories by Sara Lippmann

The Monotonous Chaos of Existence
short stories by Hisham Bustani

Peculiar Heritage
poetry DeMisty D. Bellinger

Call a Body Home
short stories chapbook by Michael Alessi

The Horror is Us
an anthology of horror fiction edited by Justin Sanders

Suppose Muscle Suppose Night Suppose This in August
memoir by Danielle Zaccagnino

Ashley Sugarnotch & the Wolf
poetry by Elizabeth Deanna Morris Lakes

Learn more at masonjarpress.com

About the Author

Photograph by Felix Kachadourian

Nancy Stohlman is the author of six books including *Madam Velvet's Cabaret of Oddities, The Vixen Scream and Other Bible Stories, The Monster Opera, Searching for Suzi,* and *Going Short: An Invitation to Flash Fiction,* which won a 2021 Reader Views Gold Award and was re-released as an audiobook in 2022. Her work has been anthologized widely, appearing in the Norton anthology *New Micro: Exceptionally Short Fiction* and *The Best Small Fictions 2019,* as well as adapted for both the stage and screen. Find her at www.nancystohlman.com.